I Am Unique!

Written by
Jennifer Vassel

Illustrated by
Penny Weber

BuddingRose Publications

I Am Unique!
By Jennifer D. Vassel

BuddingRose Publications

Illustrations by Penny Weber
Cover design by Preston K. Ayers
Interior design by Jennifer D. Vassel

Printed in the United States of America

ISBN: 0-9915556-2-7
ISBN 13: 978-0-9915556-2-8

eBook
ISBN: 978-0-9915556-4-2

Library of Congress Control Number: 2015915053
LCCN Imprint Name City and State: BuddingRose Publications - Chino Hills, CA

This Book Belongs To:

_____

Erin is a smart little girl who loves acting. She likes dressing up and rehearsing scenes from her favorite TV shows. When she grows up, she wants to be an actress.

While school is out for the summer, Erin spends most of her days pretending she's different characters—like a pirate looking for lost treasure, or a queen in her castle. She is a part of a drama club, a summer program led by her school. Erin looks forward to drama club every week because she gets to sing, dance, and play any character she chooses.

There is something unique about Erin—she was born with a birthmark by her left eye. It is the color of vanilla ice cream. She likes her birthmark because it makes her different. It makes her stand out.

Today was drama-club day, and Erin could not wait to meet with some of her friends from school. She rushed to room 458, where the club was being held. Miss Simone, the drama teacher, stood by the door and greeted the students as they walked in.

"Everyone, take your seats," she said, grinning from ear to ear. "I have a very important announcement to make!"

All the students rushed to the floor and crossed their legs. They fixed their eyes on Miss Simone. She was waving a sheet of paper in the air.

"This is such a marvelous moment!" Miss Simone was beaming. "I'm pleased to announce that we will be having our first play here at Talenton Elementary! The play is about a young princess on a magical island." All the kids started cheering.

"Auditions will be held next week in the auditorium," Miss Simone continued. "After everyone has tried out, I will have a list showing who will play each role."

Erin was so excited that she could barely contain herself. If she got the part as the princess, the entire school would see how talented she was as an actress. She could picture the audience applauding joyfully with a standing ovation. She was looking forward to audition day.

The kids chattered among themselves until Miss Simone broke up their conversations.

"OK, class! Let's get into your groups and practice your skits!"

After drama club, Erin walked out with her best friend, Madison, to wait for their parents to pick them up.

"I'm going to try out for the princess," Erin said while they walked to the parking lot. She couldn't stop smiling. "What about you, Madison?"

Madison stopped in her tracks. "You are?" she asked in surprise. "I was going to try out for that part, too."

Optimistically, Erin replied, "Well, I'd be happy if either of us got the part."

Madison looked at Erin's birthmark.

"Are you sure you want to try out for that role? I mean, princesses don't have marks on their face." She pointed to Erin's birthmark.

Erin looked at her reflection in a window nearby. "I never thought about that," she said, while tracing the outline of her birthmark. "I don't think it's a big deal. I'll think about it, though."

"Yeah, you should," Madison continued. "You wouldn't want it to distract the audience."

Erin's mom pulled up by the waiting area. Erin said good-bye to her friend, greeted her mom, and slumped into the passenger's seat. A small tear escaped her eye as they drove home. For the first time, Erin realized that her birthmark might keep her from accomplishing her dream.

Erin didn't know what to do. *Should I try out for the princess, or should I go for a smaller role where people won't notice my birthmark?*

There wasn't much time to decide. Auditions were tomorrow. Then, she got an idea.

"I know what I'm going to do!" She said out loud. "I'm still going to try out for the princess. I've got just the plan."

Erin woke up the next morning feeling energized. She leaped out of bed, washed up, and put on her clothes. Keeping her plan in mind, she tip-toed over to her parents' room. Before entering, she looked to the left and right to make sure the coast was clear.

In her parents' room, her mom had a beautiful vanity table with pretty makeup and sparkly jewelry on the countertop. She grabbed her mother's brown powder and started covering her birthmark.

No one will see my birthmark if I cover it up really well, she thought as she blotted her face with the chocolate mixture. *This way, I'll be sure to get the role as the princess!*

Just as Erin was adding the finishing touches to her face, her mother walked in, quite startled.

"Erin! What on earth are you doing?" she asked, grabbing the powder brush out of Erin's hand.

"Mommy, I was only using a little bit to cover up my birthmark!" Erin hung her head down, with shame.

"But why, Erin? Why do you want to cover your birthmark?" Her mother's voice softened.

"Because if I cover it up, I will have a better chance of getting the part as the princess."

Erin's mom's heart melted. She sat down on her bed and propped Erin up on her lap.

"Listen to me, Erin," she said in a calm voice. "Your birthmark is unique, and it's a part of who you are. You have a natural gift. You don't need to hide a part of yourself for your gifts to shine."

Erin looked into her mother's eyes and hugged her. "Thanks, Mommy," she said as she wrapped her arms around her mother's waist.

Her mother looked at her again and said, "You'll do amazing during your audition, Erin. Just be yourself. You never know who will fall in love with the person you're trying to hide."

Erin's mom got up from the bed. "Now, let's take off this makeup and get you to your audition!" They washed off the makeup, together.

Once Erin's mom dropped her off, she headed to the auditorium where auditions were taking place. Other kids were in the room waiting for Miss Simone to arrive. Erin saw Madison and greeted her pleasantly.

"Hey, Erin, you decided to try out after all?" she asked.

"Yep," Erin confirmed with confidence. "And I decided I'm going to go for the princess role. I don't care what people think about my birthmark. It makes me unique."

Before Madison could give a response, Miss Simone walked into the auditorium.

"Hello boys and girls!" she exclaimed. "Are you ready for auditions?!" The kids roared enthusiastically.

"I'll be calling a few of you at a time to recite some lines from the script," Miss Simone explained. "After we're all done, I'll take a few minutes and assign each of you a role. I'll post the list outside, and you will be able to see which role you got."

The students looked at each other, and then back at Miss Simone.

"The first group up is Ming, Ian, Gabe, and Anna!" she said.

Erin sat in the room and waited anxiously. Finally, after what seemed like several hours, Miss Simone called the next group.

"Can I have Madison, Charlie, Matthew, and…." Miss Simone scrolled up and down her roster, looking for someone to call.

"Erin! You four come with me."

Erin's heart was pounding as she walked to another room with her group. She remembered what her mom said earlier that morning: *just be yourself.*

Miss Simone handed each student his or her script. When it was Erin's turn to speak, the words flowed out of her lips like magic, and Miss Simone watched in awe.

"Well done, everyone. Now give me a few minutes to assign a role for each of you."

Erin left the room feeling proud. She was proud that she didn't have to cover up her birthmark for people to notice her natural gift of acting.

Back in the room, everyone anxiously waited for Miss Simone to post the list of roles. Just as the kids were starting to get restless, Miss Simone returned.

"OK, class, you all did an amazing job. I know you're dying to know your parts, so"—she waved a piece of paper in the air—"here they are!" She secured the paper on the wall with tape. Like a herd of cattle, the kids rushed over to the wall. Kids were jumping and screaming when they found their names.

Erin hesitantly walked over and stood on her tippy-toes to see the list over her classmates' heads. To her delight, she was listed as the princess! Shortly after, Miss Simone walked toward her.

CAST

Princess .... ERIN
Prince ...... GABE
King ...... MATTHEW
Queen .... TANYA
Fairy .... MADISON
Cow ...... CHARLIE
Judge ...... TERESA
Dragon .... KEITH
Court Jester .... ERICA

"You should be very proud of yourself, Erin," Miss Simone said while gently resting her hand on Erin's shoulder. "You have such raw talent. You'll make a great princess."

"Thank you, Miss Simone," Erin said. "I'm looking forward to learning my lines for the part." Erin was happy. She knew in her heart this was the start of great things.

The next few weeks, Erin and the rest of the cast members worked really hard, practiced their lines, and rehearsed, rehearsed, rehearsed. They also got fitted for their costumes. Miss Simone was happy the group had such great chemistry.

The day of the play finally came. The cast members stood in their places. The same nervousness Erin felt during auditions slowly crept in. Again, she remembered what her mother had said to her that one morning: *just be yourself*. The thought of her mother's words calmed her nerves. She took a deep breath.

The play started. Erin was the first on stage. She was deep in character and recited her lines with ease. The audience was immediately drawn in by her energy. Her fellow cast members flowed in—everyone blending together to tell the story.

The audience was fully engaged by each character and especially by the way Erin commanded the stage. It was breathtaking.

When the play was over, each member returned to the stage to take his or her bow. The audience whistled and applauded. Erin was the last to return to the stage, and when she did, the crowd roared and rose from their seats in unison. A standing ovation—just as she had imagined.

All the kids went offstage. Erin rushed down the stairs, through the crowd, and into her parents' arms.

"Mommy and Daddy, I did it! And no one said anything about my birthmark!"

"They wouldn't have," her dad said. "They were too focused on your talent to notice."

Erin's mom chimed in. "And even if they did notice it, your unique light shined way too bright to have been covered."

Questions to Ponder

Dear Parent, Legal Guardian, or Loved One,

I Am Unique! was written to remind young girls to love themselves just as they are and to let their natural gifts shine. While they may be able to read this book on their own, we encourage you to read it together. Below are some questions to discuss with your little one. Help keep the conversation of self-love going beyond these pages—one little girl at a time.

1. What was Erin's talent?

2. What was Erin trying to hide, and why?

3. What does it mean to be unique?

4. How was Erin unique?

5. What makes you unique?

6. What talents do you have?

7. How can you use your talents to inspire or help others?

8. Erin thought her birthmark would keep her from becoming the princess in the play. What did she learn?

9. You may not have a birthmark, but is there something you have tried to hide because you were afraid you wouldn't be accepted? What can you learn from Erin?

10. Madison questioned Erin for wanting to try out for the princess role. What will you say/do if friends, strangers, or loved ones question your dreams?

CPSIA information can be obtained at www.ICGtesting.com
Printed in the USA
BVIW12n0421160716
455412BV00008B/16